Scout   Sparkle   Arthur   Tiny

We are the Mini Monsters,
We love to laugh and play!
So join in our adventures
And have some fun – HOORAY!

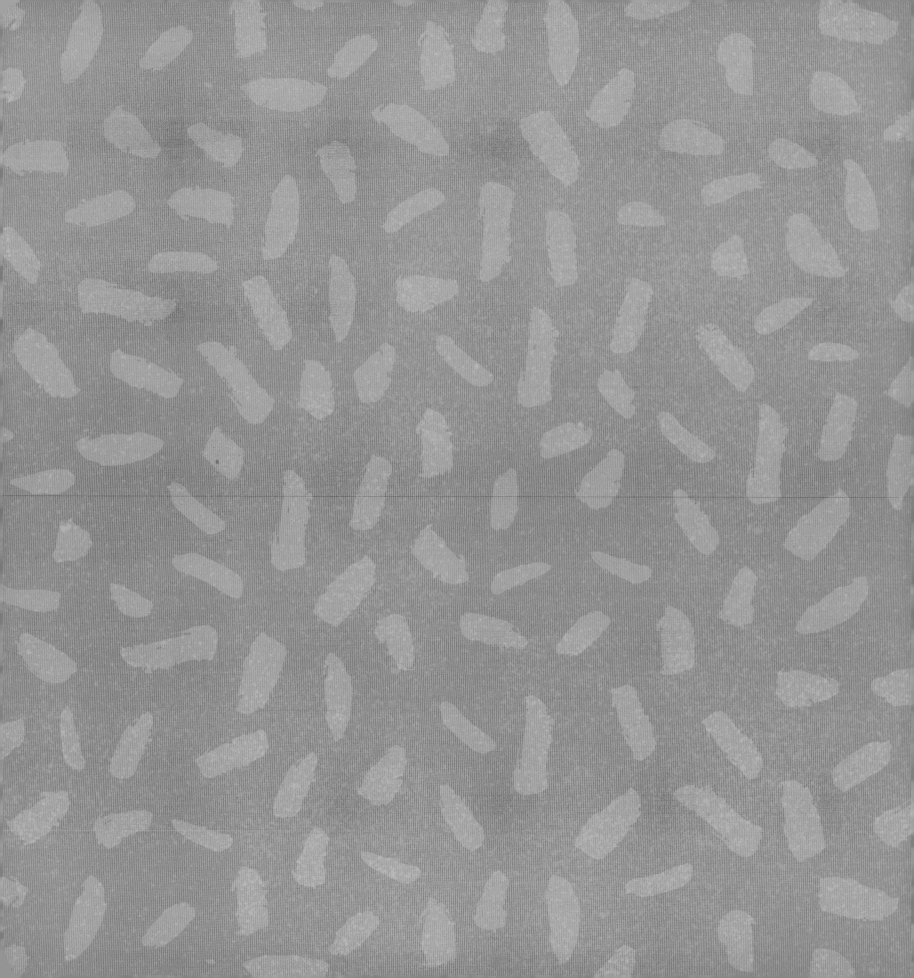

For Jess and Kat, who continue
to delight and amaze me! - CH

For Olive - TN

SIMON & SCHUSTER

First published in Great Britain in 2020 by Simon & Schuster UK Ltd
1st Floor, 222 Gray's Inn Road, London, WC1X 8HB • A CBS Company
Text copyright © 2020 Caryl Hart • Illustrations copyright © 2020 Tony Neal
The right of Caryl Hart and Tony Neal to be identified as the author and
illustrator of this work has been asserted by them in accordance with the
Copyright, Designs and Patents Act, 1988 • All rights reserved, including the
right of reproduction in whole or in part in any form • A CIP catalogue record for
this book is available from the British Library upon request.
978-1-4711-8266-2 (PB) • 978-1-4711-8268-6 (eBook)
Printed in China • 10 9 8 7 6 5 4 3 2 1

MiNi MONSTERS

Can I play?

CARYL HART & TONY NEAL

SIMON & SCHUSTER

London   New York   Sydney   Toronto   New Delhi

One day, Sparkle and Arthur were putting on a magic show.

"Oooh. Can I play? I LOVE magic!" said Scout.

Sparkle put on her top hat and gave Arthur a toy rabbit.

"You hold this and I'll make it disappear."

Scout found a floaty scarf and waved it around.

"I'm

MISTER MYSTERIOUS!"

he said.

"I need that actually!" said Sparkle.

She took the scarf from Scout and draped it over the rabbit.

Then she waved her magic wand.

"ABRACADABRA!"

But as Sparkle said the magic words...

...Arthur dropped the rabbit onto the floor.

"Arthur!"
said Sparkle.

Scout grabbed the rabbit.

"Let me try."

"No thank you, Scout.
You don't know how to
do magic and it's OUR
game, isn't it Arthur?"

"Umm,"
said Arthur.

"I'll do the trick and you be the audience," Sparkle announced.

"I'll be the audience too!"
said Scout.

Sparkle tore a bit off an old shopping list and gave it to Arthur. "There!"

Scout tried to tear off a ticket too, but Sparkle snatched the paper away.

"THIS IS **MY** SHOW AND **I** SAY **WHO** CAN WATCH!"

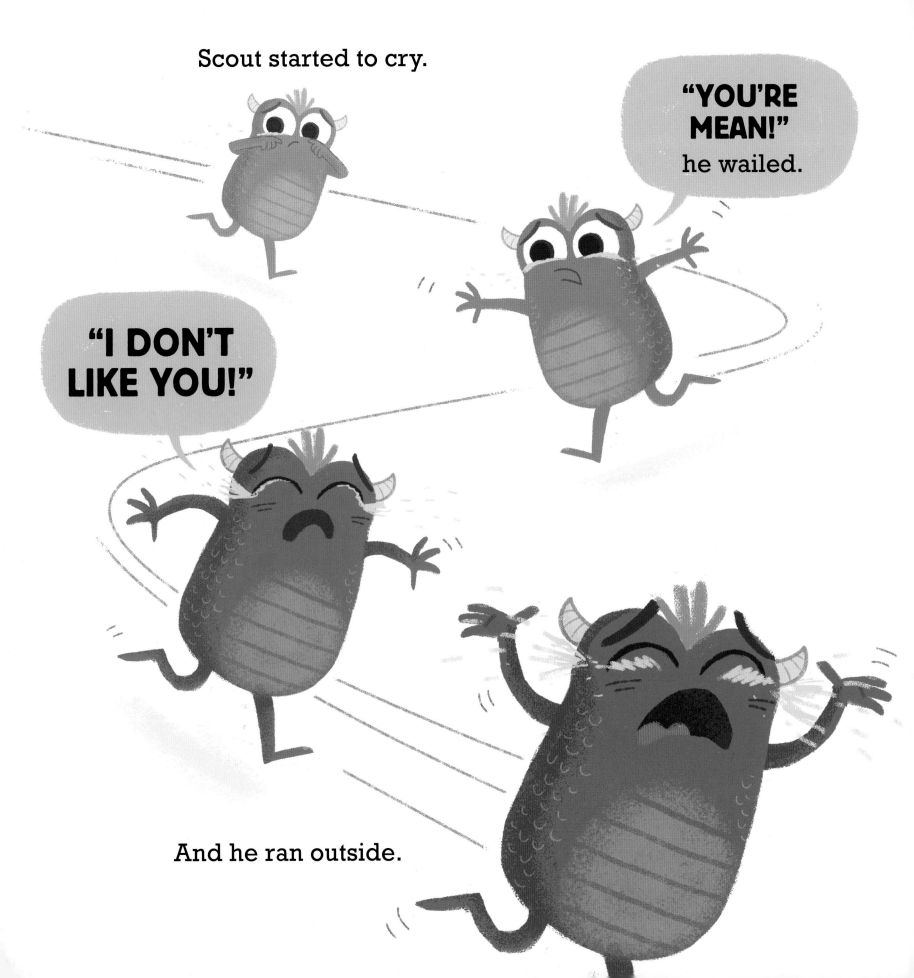

Sparkle was cross.
"I'm *not* mean!
Am I?"

"It was a *bit* mean,"
muttered Arthur and
he went to find Scout.

Sparkle stood in the middle of the stage.
Two fat tears rolled down her cheeks.

"I'm **not** mean," she sniffed.
"Arthur said he would play with *me* today and
now I don't have **anyone** to be my friend!"

Inside the playhouse, Arthur gave Scout a hug.
Sparkle watched as the two friends started a new game.

They looked so happy together.

But there was **nobody** to pick!

She tried asking Tiny, but
Tiny just tucked the card into the
cart and wheeled it away.

Sparkle felt very sad.

What was she going to do?

She found a piece
of paper and wrote
something in her
best handwriting.

Then she folded it in half
and posted it through
the playhouse door.

Back inside, Sparkle went behind
the curtains to get ready.

When she peeked out . . .

Arthur and Scout were sitting on the beanbags. They had come!
Sparkle burst through the curtains, grinning happily.

"Welcome to the
GRAND MAGIC SHOW!
I will now perform an amazing trick.
Who would like to help me?"

"Me! Me!" Scout cried.

"I think I'll choose . . .

. . . Scout!" said Sparkle.

Proudly, Scout went up to the stage.

"Pick a card, any card, and I will guess what it is," said Sparkle.

Scout picked a card and held it tight.

Sparkle tapped Scout's card three times with her magic wand.

TAP TAP TAP

"ABRACADABRA!"

she said. "Your card is . . .

...the ACE OF HEARTS!"

Scout was amazed. **"YES! YES!"** he cried. "Well done, Sparkle!"

Arthur and Tiny clapped and cheered.

Then Sparkle did a very brave thing.

"Sorry I was mean before," she said.
"I'm glad you're in my show."

Scout grinned. "You're the best friend,
and magician, ever!"

And this time, everyone agreed that
playing together was the best idea of all!

HOORAY!

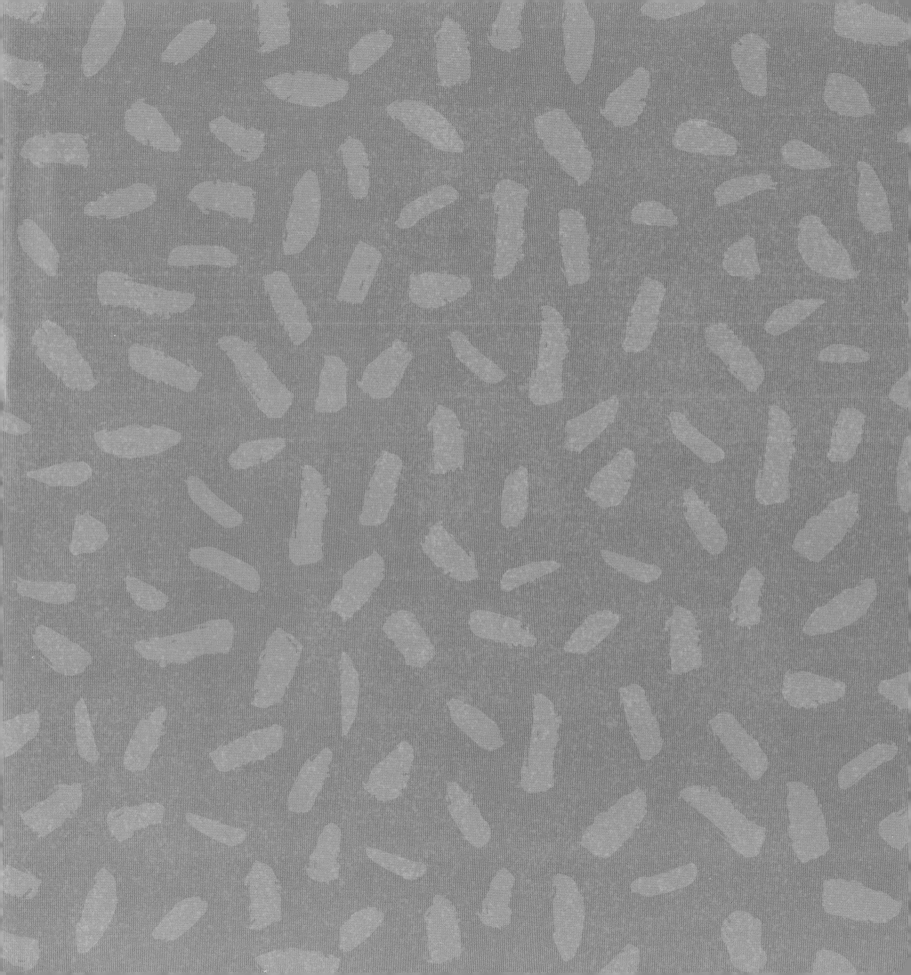